Surviving the City

Tasha Spillett

Natasha Donovan

HIGHWATER
PRESS

Canada Council   Conseil des Arts
for the Arts   du Canada

We acknowledge the support of the Canada Council for the Arts, which last year invested $153 million to bring the arts to Canadians throughout the country.

Nous remercions le Conseil des arts du Canada de son soutien. L'an dernier, le Conseil a investi 153 millions de dollars pour mettre de l'art dans la vie des Canadiennes et des Canadiens de tout le pays.

HighWater Press gratefully acknowledges the financial support of the Province of Manitoba through the Department of Sport, Culture and Heritage and the Manitoba Book Publishing Tax Credit, and the Government of Canada through the Canada Book Fund (CBF), for our publishing activities.

HighWater Press is an imprint of Portage & Main Press.
Printed and bound in Canada by Friesens
Design by Relish New Brand Experience
Cover art by Natasha Donovan
Lettering by Donovan Yaciuk
Anishinaabemowin (Saulteaux) translation: Jerry Sumner

Library and Archives Canada Cataloguing in Publication

Spillett, Tasha, 1988-, author
     Surviving the city / Tasha Spillett ; Natasha Donovan.

Issued in print and electronic formats.
ISBN 978-1-55379-756-2 (softcover).--ISBN 978-1-55379-784-5 (ebook).--
ISBN 978-1-55379-785-2 (PDF)

     1. Graphic novels. I. Donovan, Natasha, illustrator II. Title.

PN6733.S65S87 2018   j741.5'971   C2018-904204-4
                                               C2018-904205-2

21 20 19 18   1 2 3 4 5

www.highwaterpress.com
Winnipeg, Manitoba
Treaty 1 Territory and homeland of the Métis Nation

For our girls,
and the land living beneath the concrete
that remembers they are sacred.

And for the women,
seen and unseen,
who hold up the sky.
—T.S.

For my best friend, Sky – thank you for your love.
—N.D.

Little Sister

Little sister
I see you even if you have yet to see yourself
Even if you mask yourself in fragments of untruths of you
Even when you cloak yourself
because somewhere, sometime, someone has made you feel that to hide
is safer than to shine as you were meant to

Little sister
I wish to speak into your mind sacred words of you so loudly that they
are like the Thunderbirds when they come to visit
and wash everything away
I wish to make you a crown of sage to show to all that rest their eyes on you
that you are made of medicine and of royalty

Little sister
I will sing songs to you until your voice remembers that it was meant to dance
I will pray into being all that is needed to remind you
that you are where beauty and strength come together to embrace
I will dance medicine into the path that we walk on so that is again safe
for you

Little sister
I see you

OMG will this never end?

HERITAGE PR

I knooowww!
He goes on forever.

I'm starving!

Miikwan

Are you staying here
for lunch or going home?

Kokum has a doctor's
appointment, and I
don't have the house
keys. I gotta stay here 😝

Miikwan

ok let's grab pizza

ok...and i have something
to tell you.

5

HERITAGE PROJECT

AS YOU ALL KNOW, THE SCHOOL HERITAGE FAIR IS COMING UP.

FOR YOUR TERM PROJECT, YOU WILL SHARE THE PIECE OF YOUR HERITAGE THAT YOU ARE MOST PROUD OF.

YOU CAN WORK INDEPENDENTLY OR IN PAIRS.

#FreeDezsPhone

OOOOO BERRIES!! AREN'T YOU SO HAPPY WE CAN EAT THEM NOW?

REMEMBER HOW HARD IT WAS TO STAY AWAY FROM STRAWBERRY SHAKES AND HAVE PB AND J WITH NO J, FOR A WHOLE YEAR!

OUR *BERRY FAST!* THAT'S WHAT WE SHOULD DO FOR OUR HERITAGE PROJECT.

THAT'S PERFECT! WE CAN TAKE ALL THE PICTURES FROM OUR CELEBRATION FEAST OFF FACEBOOK.

KNOCK
KNOCK

HEY MY GIRL, I SAW YOUR POST ON FACEBOOK ABOUT YOUR PROJECT.

THE DRUM MOM GAVE YOU AT YOUR FEAST HASN'T BEEN BROUGHT OUT IN A WHILE.

I THINK IT'S TIME FOR IT TO SING AGAIN!

YOU SHOULD SHARE IT IN YOUR PRESENTATION.

IT'S TIME FOR US TO SING AGAIN...

DON'T STAY UP TOO LATE! YOU'VE GOT SCHOOL TOMORROW.

THANKS, DAD. LOVE YOU.

Hope everything is ok. Love you!

I GOTTA TELL YOU SOMETHING.

THE SOCIAL WORKER SAID I CAN'T STAY WITH MY KOKUM ANYMORE BECAUSE SHE'S SICK.

THEY'RE SENDING ME TO A GROUP HOME.

NO WAY! THAT'S NOT FAIR!

MY KOKUM SAYS THEY SEND LOTS OF KIDS TO GROUP HOMES NOW.

Kokum Cook
If anyone has seen @Dez, please call me asap. She didn't make it home yesterday...

SHE'S MY BEST FRIEND. WE'RE LIKE SISTERS.

WE'RE SO CLOSE, WE EVEN GOT OUR FIRST MOON TIMES IN THE SAME MONTH! WE DID OUR BERRY FAST TOGETHER.

WHEN IT WAS TIME TO BREAK OUR FAST, HER KOKUM GAVE US OUR FIRST BITE OF BERRIES.

MY MOM WAS STILL WITH US THEN...

OH, MY GIRL, EVERYONE WAS AND STILL IS SO PROUD OF YOU GIRLS!

COMPLETING YOUR BERRY FAST IS A GREAT ACCOMPLISHMENT.

BEING CELEBRATED AS A VALUED PART OF OUR CIRCLE IS AN EXPERIENCE THAT YOU CAN ALWAYS LEAN ON.

I KNOW YOU'RE SCARED RIGHT NOW.

OUR TEACHINGS TELL US THAT IN TIMES LIKE THIS, WE CAN MAKE AN OFFERING, SO THAT OUR ANCESTORS COME STAND WITH US.

DO YOU WANT TO DO THAT?

SNIFF

YA, OKAY.

I WANNA GO HOME... BUT MY PHONE'S DEAD, AND I HAVE NO BUS FARE.

WERE YOU OUT HERE ALL NIGHT?

YA. I DIDN'T KNOW WHERE TO GO.

YOU GOTTA BE CAREFUL OUT HERE. IT CAN GET PRETTY ROUGH IN THE CITY.

I KNOW SOMEWHERE YOU CAN USE THE PHONE AND MAYBE GET SOME BUS TICKETS.

I DON'T WANT TO GO ANYWHERE MY SOCIAL WORKER WILL FIND ME. SHE'S TRYING TO TAKE ME AWAY FROM MY KOKUM.

IT'S NOT LIKE THAT THERE. IT'S COMMUNITY ORGANIZATION RUN BY OUR PEOPLE. THEY CAN HELP YOU HOME TO YOUR KOKUM. YOU CAN EVEN HAVE A GOOD SMUDGE. CAN WALK WITH YOU IF YOU WANT.

I DON'T KNOW--

IT'S BETTER TO BE WITH COMMUNITY THAN OUT HERE ON YOUR OWN, MY GIRL.

MY KOKUM ALWAYS USED TO SAY KAKIYAW NIWAHKOMAKANAK--WE ARE ALL RELATED. SOMETIMES, WE NEED TO LEAN ON ONE ANOTHER FOR SUPPORT. IT'S OKAY TO NEED ONE ANOTHER.

IF THEY CAN HELP ME GET HOME TO MY KOKUM, I'LL CHECK IT OUT.

THUNDERBIRD HOUSE

ANIIN.*
TOMORROW IS OUR MARCH IN HONOUR OF OUR BELOVED MOTHERS, AUNTIES, SISTERS, AND FRIENDS.

THIS EVENING, WE'LL FINISH OUR PREPARATIONS BY MAKING THE BEAUTIFUL SIGNS THAT WE CARRY WITH US EVERY YEAR.

*HELLO

THANK YOU FOR COMING, EVERYONE.

THESE BUTTERFLIES WILL HELP REMIND EVERYONE THAT OUR WOMEN ARE MORE THAN THE STATISTICS, THAT THEY ARE VALUED AND LOVED.

YOU'RE ALL WELCOME TO SMUDGE WITH ME BEFORE YOU GO HOME.

HEY GIRL, GET IN! I'LL GIVE YOU A RIDE WHEREVER YOU WANNA GO.

NO. MY BUS IS COMING RIGHT AWAY.

YOU'RE SAFE. YOU'RE HOME.

LOVE YOU, SIS.

Miikwan
Just now
Sisters 4ever 🖤

Murdered and Missing Indigenous Women, Girls, and Two-Spirit People

By Tasha Spillett

As a direct consequence of colonialism, settler capitalism, racism, misogyny, and other forms of oppression, Indigenous women, girls, and two-spirit people are among the most marginalized populations in Canada and globally. We face a greater risk of experiencing racialized and gender-based violence, being murdered, or going missing.

As a part of our refusal of victimhood and in the spirit of resistance, Indigenous women and two-spirit people lead movements against the violence that puts our lives at risk while also healing our communities from the losses we've experienced.

Indigenous women and two-spirit people affirm that our lives are valuable and that we have the right to live on our homelands with respect and dignity, free from violence.

Statistics About MMIWG2S

Indigenous women are five times more likely to be murdered than non-Indigenous women.[1] However, Statistics Canada and several major police forces do not track missing Indigenous women;[2] therefore the following disturbing statistics can only be considered estimates lower than the actual numbers.

According to the Native Women's Association of Canada (NWAC):[3]

- Based on 582 cases of missing and murdered Indigenous women, just over half of the cases (55%) involve women and girls under the age of 31, with 17% of women and girls 18 years of age or younger.
- Nearly half the murder cases in NWAC's database remain unsolved.
- Indigenous women are almost three times more likely to be killed by a stranger than non-Indigenous women.

Of the murder cases in NWAC's database where someone has been charged:

- 16.5% of offenders are strangers with no prior connection to the woman or girl (in contrast, Statistics Canada reports that, between 1997 and 2004, only 6% of murdered non-Indigenous women were killed by strangers);
- 17% of offenders are acquaintances of the woman or girl (a friend, neighbour or someone else known to her); and
- 23% of offenders are a current or former partner of the woman or girl.

According to a 2015 report from the RCMP:[4]

- 10% of women in Canada missing for at least 30 days are Indigenous women.

---

1   David, Jean-Denis. "Homicide in Canada, 2016." Statistics Canada (website), accessed October 24, 2018, https://www150.statcan.gc.ca/n1/pub/85-002-x/2017001/article/54879-eng.htm

2   Margo McDiarmid, "Still no way to tell how many Indigenous women and girls go missing in Canada each year," CBC (website), CBC News, December 20, 2017, https://www.cbc.ca/news/politics/indigenous-missing-women-police-data-1.4449073.

3   "Fact Sheet: Missing and Murdered Aboriginal Women and Girls," Native Women's Association of Canada (website), Native Women's Association of Canada, accessed October 23, 2018, https://www.nwac.ca/wp-content/uploads/2015/05/Fact_Sheet_Missing_and_Murdered_Aboriginal_Women_and_Girls.pdf.

4   "Missing and Murdered Indigenous Women and Girls," Department of Justice (website), Department of Justice, accessed October 23, 2018, http://justice.gc.ca/eng/rp-pr/jr/jf-pf/2017/july04.html.

- Of these, nearly two-thirds were identified as missing due to "unknown" circumstances, or foul play was suspected.
- Between 1980 and 2014, there were 6,849 police-reported female homicide cases in Canada. 16% of the victims were Indigenous women.
- Since 1991, the number of murdered non-Indigenous women has declined. In contrast, the number of murdered Indigenous women has remained relatively stable, thus accounting for an increasing proportion of Indigenous female homicide victims.

More About MMIWG2S

Altamirano-Jiménez, Isabel. "Indigenous women, nationalism and feminism." *States of Race: Critical Race Feminism for the 21st Century*, edited by S. Razak, M. Smith and S. Thobani, 111-126. Toronto: Between the Lines, 2010.

Beads, Tina and Rauna Kuokkanen. "An Aboriginal Feminist on Violence against Women." *Making Space for Indigenous Feminism*, edited by Joyce Green, 221-232. Winnipeg: Fernwood Publishing, 2007.

Bourassa, Carrie, Kim McKay-McNabb, and Mary Hampton. (2004). "Racism, Sexism and Colonialism: The Impact on the Health of Aboriginal Women in Canada." *Canadian Woman Studies*, 24, no. 1 (2005), 23-29.

Brant, Jennifer and Dawn Memee Lavall-Harvard, *Forever Loved: Exposing the Hidden Crisis of Missing and Murdered Indigenous Women and Girls in Canada*. Bradford, ON: Demeter Press, 2016.

Kuokkanen, Rauna. "Confronting violence: Indigenous women, Self-determination and International Human Rights." *Indivisible: Indigenous Human Rights*, edited by Joyce Green, 126-143. Winnipeg: Fernwood Press, 2014.

Palmater, Pam. "The Law's Role in Canada's Disgrace: Murdered & Missing Indigenous Women & Girls" EquitableEducation. Retrieved October 23, 2018: https://www.youtube.com/watch?v=6g665LSQpX0.

"Stolen Sisters: A Human Rights Response to Discrimination and Violence against Indigenous Women in Canada," Amnesty International (website), Amnesty International, accessed October 23, 2018, https://www.amnesty.ca/sites/amnesty/files/amr200032004enstolensisters.pdf.

Tuck, Eve and K. Wayne Yang (2012). "Decolonization is not a metaphor." *Decolonization: Indigeneity, Education & Society*, 1 no. 1 (2012), 1-40.

"Violence Against Indigenous Women and Girls in Canada: A Summary of Amnesty International's Concerns and Call to Action," Amnesty International (website), Amnesty International, last modified February 7, 2014, https://www.amnesty.ca/sites/amnesty/files/iwfa_submission_amnesty_international_february_2014_-_final.pdf.

Walker, Connie, "Who Killed Alberta Williams," CBC Radio (website), CBC Radio, February 24, 2015, https://www.cbc.ca/news/politics/indigenous-missing-women-police-data-1.4449073.

Further Reading

Adams, K.C. *Perception Photo Series*. Winnipeg, MB: HighWater Press, 2019.

Clements, Marie. *The Edward Curtis Project: A Modern Picture Story*. Vancouver, BC: Talonbooks, 2010.

Dimaline, Cherie. *The Marrow Thieves*. Toronto, ON: Dancing Cat Books, 2017.

Dumont, Marilyn. *A Really Good Brown Girl*. London, ON: Brick Books, 2015.

Justice, Daniel Heath. *The Way of Thorn & Thunder, Vol. 1-3*. Neyaashiinigmiing, ON: Kegedonce Press, 2016.

Mosionier, Beatrice. *In Search of April Raintree*. Winnipeg, MB: Portage & Main Press, 2008.

Robertson, David A. *Betty: The Helen Betty Osborne Story*. Winnipeg, MB: HighWater Press, 2016.

Robertson, David A. *Will I See?* Winnipeg, MB: HighWater Press, 2017.

Storm, Jennifer. *Deadly Loyalties*. Penticton, BC: Theytus Books, 2007.

Taylor, Drew Hayden. *The Night Wanderer: A Graphic Novel*. Toronto, ON: Annick Press, 2013.

Vermette, Katherena. *A Girl Called Echo, Vol. 1-4*. Winnipeg, MB: HighWater Press, 2017-2020.